my cat
likes to hide
in
boxes

Spindlewood

by Eve Sutton
illustrated by Lynley Dodd

My cat likes to hide in boxes.

The cat from France
Liked to sing and dance.

But MY cat likes to hide in boxes.

The cat from Spain
Flew an aeroplane.
The cat from France
Liked to sing and dance.

But MY cat likes to hide in boxes.

The cat from Norway
Got stuck in the doorway.
The cat from Spain
Flew an aeroplane.
The cat from France
Liked to sing and dance.

But MY cat likes to hide in boxes.

The cat from Greece
Joined the police.
The cat from Norway
Got stuck in the doorway.
The cat from Spain
Flew an aeroplane.
The cat from France
Liked to sing and dance.

But MY cat likes to hide in boxes.

The cat from Brazil
Caught a very bad chill.
The cat from Greece
Joined the police.
The cat from Norway
Got stuck in the doorway.
The cat from Spain
Flew an aeroplane.
The cat from France
Liked to sing and dance.

But MY cat likes to hide in boxes.

The cat from Berlin
Played the violin.
The cat from Brazil
Caught a very bad chill.
The cat from Greece
Joined the police.
The cat from Norway
Got stuck in the doorway.
The cat from Spain
Flew an aeroplane.
The cat from France
Liked to sing and dance.

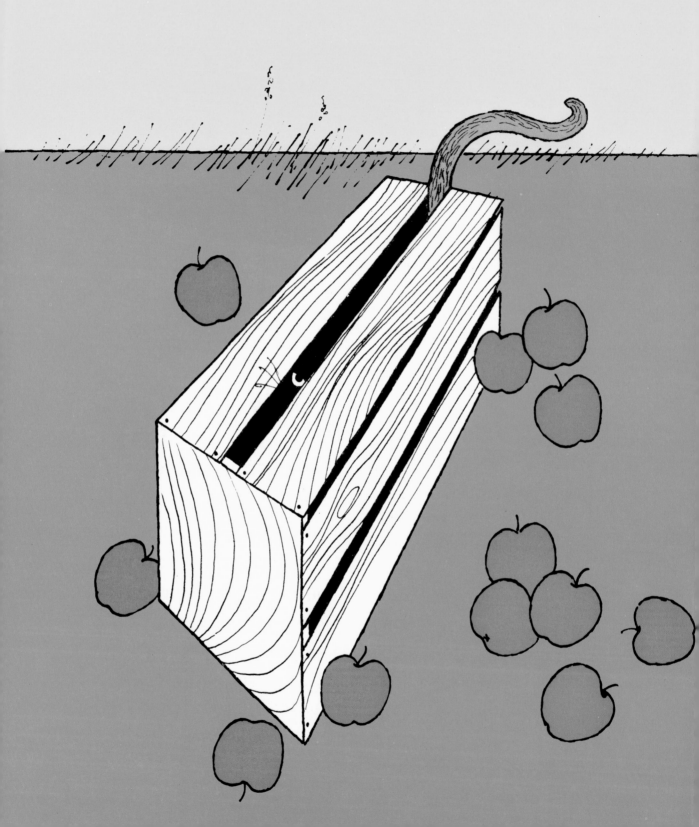

But MY cat likes to hide in boxes.

The cat from Japan
Waved a big blue fan.
The cat from Berlin
Played the violin.
The cat from Brazil
Caught a very bad chill.
The cat from Greece
Joined the police.
The cat from Norway
Got stuck in the doorway.
The cat from Spain
Flew an aeroplane.
The cat from France
Liked to sing and dance.

Look at all these clever cats,
Cats from Spain, Brazil and France,
Cats from Greece, Japan and Norway,
Cats who sing and fly and dance . . .

BUT MY CAT LIKES TO HIDE IN BOXES.

Other Lynley Dodd books

THE NICKLE NACKLE TREE
TITIMUS TRIM
THE APPLE TREE
THE SMALLEST TURTLE
HAIRY MACLARY FROM DONALDSON'S DAIRY
HAIRY MACLARY'S BONE
HAIRY MACLARY SCATTERCAT
WAKE UP, BEAR
HAIRY MACLARY'S CATERWAUL CAPER
A DRAGON IN A WAGON
HAIRY MACLARY'S RUMPUS AT THE VET
SLINKY MALINKI
FIND ME A TIGER

British Library Cataloguing in Publication Data

Sutton, Eve
  My cat likes to hide in boxes.
  1. Title
  823'.914[J] PZ7

Published in Great Britain in 1984 by Spindlewood,
70 Lynhurst Avenue, Barnstaple, Devon EX31 2HY.

First published in Great Britain in 1973
by Hamish Hamilton Children's Books Ltd.
This edition first published in New Zealand
in 1984 by Mallinson Rendel Publishers Ltd,
P.O. Box 9409, Wellington.

Reprinted February 1985
Reprinted 1986
Reprinted May 1987
Reprinted June 1989
Reprinted July 1991
Reprinted June 1993

ISBN 0-907349-70-6

Printed by Colorcraft Ltd., Hong Kong